For Little Miss Violet

Nicholas Callaway, Editorial Director
Antoinette White, Senior Editor • Toshiya Masuda, Designer • True Sims, Production Director
Paula Litzky, Director of Sales and Marketing • Jeremy Ross, Director of New Technology • Roman Milisic, Assistant Editor
Ivan Wong, Jr. and José Rodríguez, Design and Production Associates
With thanks to Jennifer Braunstein at Scholastic Press and to Debbie Geri, Personal Assistant, and Raphael Shea, Art Assistant, at David Kirk's studio.

Library of Congress Cataloging-in-Publication Data
Kirk, David, 1955–
Little Miss Spider at Sunny Patch School/paintings and verse by David Kirk
p. cm.
Summary: On her first day at school, Little Miss Spider worries that she cannot do what the others can, but she learns that she has a special quality all her own.
ISBN 0-439-08727-9
[1. Spiders—Fiction. 2. Insects—Fiction. 3. First day of school—Fiction. 4. Schools—Fiction. 5. Stories in rhyme.]
I. Title.
PZ8.3.K6554Lo   2000
[E]—dc21   99-056671
CIP   AC
10 9 8 7 6 5 4 3 2 1   9/9 0/0 1 2 3 4

Printed in China by Palace Press International
First edition, September 2000

The paintings in this book are oils on paper.

Little Miss Spider

at Sunny Patch School

paintings and verse by David Kirk

Scholastic Press

Callaway

New York

Little Miss Spider
Got ready for school.
She packed her new notebook,
Her pencils and rule.

Peering outside,

She sipped tea from her cup

And eagerly watched

For the sun to come up!

She dreamt as she gazed,

Her mind running through

The wonderful things

She would learn how to do.

Sunny Patch School
Was the best place to go
To study the lessons
All bugs ought to know.

There were classes in climbing
And clinging to walls,
For hiding in bushes
And curling in balls.

She would learn about flowers,
From petal to root—
How to chew tasty leaves
And tunnel through fruit.

She gobbled her breakfast—
A fresh flower plate,
Then ran the whole way
To be first at the gate.

The principal smiled
As he pulled back the latch,
"I know you'll be happy
At dear Sunny Patch!"

But she found she lacked talent
For hiding in trees,
For chirping like crickets
Or humming like bees.

She hadn't the strength
To drill leaves with her tongue,
And hardly the stomach
For digging in dung.

"I am useless at stinging,"
She said with a sigh.
"Perhaps I'll be better
At learning to fly."

Each student was tossed
From the leaf of a rose.
Poor Little Miss Spider
Fell flat on her nose.

The school day was over.
They sounded the bell.
She sobbed, "Is there *anything*
I can do well?"

Then she heard a bug cry,
"I'm stuck in a spout!"
So she climbed to the top,
And she hoisted him out.

The principal beamed,
As he watched from afar.
He lifted Miss Spider
And gave her a star.

"Our gifts, they are many:
We hop, fly, and crawl.
But kindness," he said,
"Is the finest of all!"